WITHDRAWN

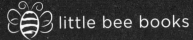 little bee books

251 Park Avenue South, New York, NY 10010
Copyright © 2019 by Little Bee Books
All rights reserved, including the right of
reproduction in whole or in part in any form.
Manufactured in China RRD 0520
ISBN: 978-1-4998-0824-7 (pbk)
First Edition 10 9 8 7 6 5 4 3 2
ISBN: 978-1-4998-0825-4 (hc)
First Edition 10 9 8 7 6 5 4 3 2 1
ISBN: 978-1-4998-0826-1 (ebook)

Library of Congress Cataloging-in-Publication Data
is available upon request.

For more information about special discounts on bulk purchases,
please contact Little Bee Books at sales@littlebeebooks.com.

littlebeebooks.com

Isle of MISFITS
THE MISSING POT OF GOLD

by JAMIE MAE
illustrated by FREYA HARTAS

little bee books

CONTENTS

—— CHAPTER ONE ——

READY TO ROLL

When Gibbon and his friends earned their very first mission to help another creature in trouble, he didn't think it would start with them in a classroom. Wasn't the whole point of going on a mission to get away from the academy? Gibbon tapped his claw against his desk as he waited for the professor to arrive.

Ebony, of course, sat in the very front of the room. She eagerly arranged her colorful pens and notebooks on her desk. Fiona sighed loudly as she fluttered around, filled with too much energy to stay still.

Gibbon sat in the middle, bored as he stared at the clock. Yuri was behind him, snoring away.

Suddenly, the door burst open. Yuri sat up straight and Fiona darted over to her desk as Fitzgerald entered the classroom.

"You've got a great mission!" he announced as he walked in.

Ebony flipped open one of her notebooks and picked up a pen to start taking notes.

"You're going to Ireland," Fitzgerald explained. "You'll be helping a leprechaun by the name of Declan find his missing pot of gold."

"Leprechauns?" Fiona whined. "Seriously?"

Yuri perked up. "What's wrong with leprechauns?"

"Have you ever *met* a leprechaun?" Fiona muttered.

Yuri shook his head, looking at Gibbon and Alistair. Both of them shrugged.

"Just wait," she grumbled. "You'll see what I mean. Or smell, at least."

"Now, now," Fitzgerald said, "a leprechaun's gold is their whole life savings. If you don't find it, he'll have nothing. You'll have to look for clues, decode their meanings, and piece it all together to figure out what happened. Now if you're all ready, follow me."

Gibbon leapt to his feet. Ireland! A whole new adventure with his friends!

5

When they arrived at the leprechaun village, Gibbon was in awe. It was unlike any place he could have ever imagined. Apparently, leprechauns were tiny little creatures with brightly colored hair and big, booming laughs. They bustled about the town filled with mushroom homes and shops built into trees. He didn't remember much about leprechauns except that they had something to do with being lucky? Or gold? Or maybe something to do with a rainbow?

Fiona grumbled as she waved her hand in front of her nose. "Leprechauns always smell like mud. It's like they bathe in the stuff. *Ugh!* Someone needs to teach them about the wonders of soap and water."

"Oh, hush," Ebony replied. Her big, black eyes scanned the village like it was a treat she couldn't wait to devour.

"Everything's so . . . tiny," Alistair whispered, rubbing his claws against the back of his neck. He was so much larger than everything else around him. One wrong step and he might accidentally stomp someone's home completely flat. Considering how clumsy Alistair was, it was a real risk.

Gibbon knew his friend was clumsy, but it was Fiona he was really worried about. He'd thought she'd be happy to be back in her homeland of Ireland, but he could never really tell what would rub Fiona's fiery temper the wrong way.

"Where do you think Declan lives?" Yuri wondered aloud.

"Declan?" a nearby leprechaun laughed. His friend joined him and they shook their heads over cups of tea they poured out of a mushroom pot. "You mean Scatterbrains? Lost his pot of gold again, did he?"

"Does that happen a lot—hey, what's your name?" Ebony inquired.

The leprechaun eyed Ebony, like she was a strange sight. Gibbon guessed that, to them, a griffin probably looked weird. Fiona was the only creature in the group they were used to seeing.

"The name's Rory, and this here is Liam. Declan is a bit . . ." Rory frowned as he stroked his long, green beard.

"Declan's missing a few pieces up here," Liam said, tapping the side of his head. "He's lost his pot of gold four times in just the last year alone. Always forgetting which rainbow he put it under, I tell ya'. It's never *really* lost."

"Give him a week and he'll remember where he put it," said Rory.

"See, Fitz?" Fiona muttered. "He probably just misplaced it or something."

Fitzgerald crossed his arms. "I admit, Declan isn't the most reliable source, but this time he's sure someone took his gold. Your job is to find out what happened and get it back to him."

"We've got this!" Yuri declared as he high-fived Alistair.

Gibbon laughed, but he noticed that Ebony looked uncertain. And Fiona looked downright annoyed.

It'll be okay, he thought. *We're ready!*

THE GOOFBALL

—— GIBBON ——
HEIGHT: 2.2 feet
WEIGHT: 176 pounds
STRENGTH: Optimistic
WEAKNESS: Unable to sit still
BIGGEST FEAR: Humans
FAVORITE FOOD: Candy canes

—— FIONA ——
HEIGHT: 7 inches
WEIGHT: 1.02 pounds
STRENGTH: Cunning
WEAKNESS: Unstable temper
BIGGEST FEAR: None
FAVORITE FOOD: Tears

THE TOUGH ONE

THE BRAINS

—— EBONY ——
HEIGHT: 6 feet, 10 inches
WEIGHT: 399 pounds
STRENGTH: Super-smart
WEAKNESS: Poor flying skills
BIGGEST FEAR: Failing classes
FAVORITE FOOD: Peanut butter
& jelly sandwiches

—— YURI ——
HEIGHT: 8 feet, 2 inches
WEIGHT: 476 pounds
STRENGTH: Tying a man bun
WEAKNESS: Tropical climates
BIGGEST FEAR: Naked mole-rats
FAVORITE FOOD: Artichokes

THE LEADER

THE KLUTZ

—— ALISTAIR ——
HEIGHT: 16 feet
WEIGHT: 1.5 tons
STRENGTH: Fire-breathing
WEAKNESS: Clumsy
BIGGEST FEAR: Knights in
shining armor
FAVORITE FOOD: Anything
charred

THE MISSING
POT OF GOLD

CHAPTER TWO

REALLY SMELLY LEPRECHAUNS

Declan's house was made out of a big, red mushroom located right below an ancient tree. Upon entering it, his home looked like a bomb of clothes and pots went off in it, which made Ebony think the leprechauns in town had been right about Declan. He *was* scatterbrained.

Maybe he really had just put his pot of gold under the wrong rainbow?

Ebony watched as Declan ran around his kitchen, trying to find teacups. He wanted to serve them tea as they talked, but so far, he hadn't been able to find anything but a few pots and pans.

"I know I have cups here somewhere. . . ." Declan muttered to himself.

Yep, completely unorganized, Ebony thought.

"Just tell us what happened already!" Fiona squeaked.

Yuri and Gibbon had sat on the couch in the living room. Yuri had to hunch over to avoid hitting his head on the ceiling. Alistair had to poke his head in through the window since he was far too large to fit inside the mushroom house.

"Right!" Declan closed his kitchen cabinets and turned toward them. "I went to the end of the south rainbow; it's the one that you can see directly over town. I *know* I left my pot of gold there—"

"We were told that you forget which rainbow you leave your gold under all the time," Yuri said. His ice-blue eyes watched Declan.

Good point, Ebony thought. She wished she had brought that up, but she was too nervous to speak. She kept having thoughts like . . . *What if I'm bad at piecing together clues? What if I ask the wrong questions? What if the team would be better off without me?*

"No, this time I *know* I left it under the south rainbow!" Declan declared hotly. "Besides, when I went to check on my gold, the pot was still there. But now, it's empty! You can go and see for yourselves."

"Oh, trust us. We will!" Fiona said. "Do you know how common it is for a leprechaun to leave gold at the end of a rainbow? It's like you were asking for someone to steal it."

Declan frowned. "Where else would I leave my gold then?"

"A secret room in a castle!" Gibbon suggested. "It always worked for me."

"No—a treasure box deep in a cave," Alistair chimed in.

"Those would have been better places," Declan said as his shoulders sagged. His attention shifted up to the ceiling, which was drooping in the center. Between that and the creak of the floorboards, Ebony guessed he needed to do some repairs.

"Don't worry, Declan. We're here to help you," Ebony said.

"Yeah, we'll find it!" Gibbon stood up and placed his hands on his hips like he was a superhero.

Even if she had her doubts about her own abilities, Ebony believed Gibbon. Her team hadn't let her down yet, and she wasn't about to let down Declan, either.

CHAPTER THREE

WHERE LEPRECHAUNS REALLY HIDE THEIR GOLD

Yuri had suggested that they start by questioning other leprechauns around the village. Alistair was glad to start searching for some real clues.

But none of us know what we're doing, he realized. Yuri liked to pretend he knew the best place to start, but deep down, none of them had ever done this before.

If Ebony had spoken up and said something, Alistair would have believed her without a doubt. She was, after all, the smartest creature in their whole group. Their whole academy even.

But she was following along with their plans, whispering about how she hoped she didn't get anything wrong.

To Alistair, Ireland smelled fresh— like trees and flowers and berries. The leprechauns didn't smell as nice, but since the dragon was by far the biggest creature in the village, his head was closer to the beautiful trees.

None of the leprechauns seemed like they enjoyed having the misfits in their town. The first three leprechauns they tried to talk to ran away. Finally, they came across a leprechaun with bright pink hair. Gibbon asked if she would answer some questions, and she grunted and shrugged in reply.

"That's a yes," Fiona muttered. "Leprechauns aren't wordy."

"Little fairy thinks she knows what's what, does she now?" the pink leprechaun asked, glaring.

"Hey, who are you calling 'little'?" Fiona flew up to the leprechaun. Even compared with these small creatures, Fiona was still super-small. Smaller than Alistair's claws.

He loved his friend, but he also worried that he'd accidentally squash her if he wasn't careful. *It's not always fun being the biggest creature around*, he thought.

"Okay, okay." Yuri stepped between the two fierce girls. "We're sorry, ma'am. Do you know Declan? We're trying to help him find his gold."

The leprechaun sighed and shook her head. "Don't ma'am me, child! Name's Beth. And aye, I heard Declan lost his gold again. Poor fella, this is—what? The fourth time this year?"

"Yeah, we've heard it's happened a few times already," Ebony said sadly.

A big laugh left the leprechaun, bigger and louder than anything Alistair had ever heard. "Oh, it's been a lot more than a few! You know what his biggest problem is?"

"What?" Gibbon asked curiously.

"He still puts it at the end of a rainbow. Can you believe that?"

"Well, where do you keep *your* gold then?" Ebony asked.

"Ha, ha, *ha*, young lassie," Beth said with a firm shake of her head. "I'm not about to tell you that! How do I know you won't go stealing it?"

"We're here to *help* a leprechaun find his missing gold, not take anyone else's," Alistair said.

Beth looked from Ebony back to Alistair with narrowed eyes. "How about this? I'll tell you some places I've heard *other* leprechauns hide their gold?"

"Yes, thank you!" Ebony said.

"One bloke puts his in a hollowed-out tree, though he does have to worry about squirrels getting at it. Another gal hides hers in her gym locker because no one in their right mind would want to go near that awful stench. And a fella I know keeps his buried in his garden. He planted some pretty flowers above it, so he could remember where it was."

With that, Beth wandered off. Maybe Declan *had* left his pot somewhere else and simply forgot. Alistair could sympathize with his situation. He had done that before with some of his things, too. One of the good things about having a roommate was having a friend who could help him find lost things now.

"We should split up," Yuri said. "Ebony and Alistair, you fly to the end of the south rainbow and look for Declan's gold there. The rest of us will search the forest nearby and try to think of other places he might have left his gold—"

"I don't want to go running all around Ireland," Fiona whined.

Yuri sighed, the bun on the top of his head bobbing as he did. "Okay . . . how about you stay with Declan then?"

"That's not what I had in mind," she grumbled.

"Well, you could look around his place while you're there—see if he left his gold somewhere inside the house. How's that sound?"

A smile formed at the edge of her lips. "So, I'd be like a spy?"

Yuri smirked. "Yup! A secret fairy spy."

CHAPTER FOUR

THE FIRST CLUE

Yuri and Gibbon left to explore the forest. It was a little cold in Ireland, but Yuri liked that. He was from a naturally cold climate, and the Isle of Misfits was a little warmer than what he was used to. He missed the snow, so the gray chill in Ireland felt nice.

As they wandered through the forest, he looked at the ground and also at the tops of the trees, trying to find any clues as to where Declan might have hidden his gold. After checking all the bushes and hollowed-out trees they could find, they came up with nothing.

Gibbon kicked a twig on the ground. "How haven't we found any clues?"

Yuri shrugged. This mission wasn't as exciting as he had hoped, but at least they were helping someone. That's what was important.

"I know it's not the most fun," Yuri said, turning to Gibbon. "But we wouldn't be proving ourselves if we fail this mission. And Declan, scatterbrained as he might be, really does need our help."

"I guess you're right," Gibbon said with a sigh.

Together, they kept searching the forest. They walked through an open field and across a stream. Once again, it led to nothing. Maybe Yuri had been wrong about searching the forest?

What would Fitzgerald do in my situation? Gibbon wondered.

"Yuri! Yuri! I found something!"

Yuri jumped up in surprise and ran over to his friend, who held a pot of gold in his hands. He danced around, jiggling the gold as he did. Yuri was ready to start dancing, too! Until he saw the coins. His face fell.

"Wait . . . That isn't Declan's. . . ."

Gibbon frowned and stopped dancing. "How do you know that?"

Yuri reached in and picked up a piece of gold. It had a leprechaun's face on it, but it was a girl! "Leprechauns put their faces on their gold, so they know which is theirs. This isn't Declan's face."

"Oh." Gibbon dropped the pot with a thud.

"Come on, put it back where
you found it and let's keep
searching." Yuri said.

Just when they were about to give up, they came across a very dark and still lake. It seemed so big, Yuri couldn't see land on the other side of it.

"Let's rest here," Yuri suggested as he sat down and dipped his feet into the lake. Yuri sighed with relief. The chill of the water felt so nice. When Gibbon didn't join him, he looked over to see his friend staring nervously at the water. "What's wrong?"

"I can't swim," Gibbon muttered. "At least, I don't think so. I've never tried. But I'm pretty sure I'd sink to the bottom like a stone. You know, because I *am* stone."

Yuri chuckled and patted the grass beside him. "Don't worry, this is the shallow part of the lake. You could stand in the water here and it'd only come up to your waist!"

Gibbon looked at the water one more time before he slowly walked over and sat down next to Yuri. Once he dipped his feet in, his shoulders relaxed and he smiled. "This isn't so bad."

"Told you so." Yuri grinned.

Something bright in the water caught Yuri's eye. He squinted and looked harder—was he imaging it? No! When the sun broke through the gray clouds, something definitely shimmered in the water.

"Gibbon, do you see that?"

Gibbon looked where Yuri was pointing. "I do!" He stepped down into the water. For a second, he froze like he was too scared to go any farther. But then Gibbon took a half step forward. Then another. With each step, Gibbon looked a little more relaxed. With the water up to his waist, he leaned down and picked up a piece of gold off the bottom of the lake. "Is this Declan?"

Yuri took it from Gibbon and examined it. It was *definitely* Declan's face on the coin. "It is! We've found the gold! Though, uh . . . where's the rest of it?"

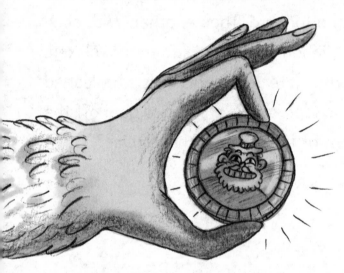

Something big moved in the water behind Gibbon. It went by so quickly though, Yuri didn't know if it was a bird's shadow or if there was something else in the water with them.

Yuri looked around, but he didn't see anything else shimmer in the sunlight. If one piece glimmered enough for them to see it through the dark water, he was pretty sure other pieces would've been noticeable, too. "Do you see anything?"

Gibbon glanced around. "Nope. Maybe whoever took the gold only passed through here and dropped one coin?"

"Let's go show this to the others," Yuri suggested. He didn't know what was in the water. Maybe it was just his imagination, but he didn't want to stick around to find out.

FRIGHTFUL FLYING

Ebony was terrified. Completely terrified. Her whole body shook as she and Alistair walked to the edge of town. Alistair had wanted to take off right away, but she had talked him out of it. She said it would be easier if they got the edge of town first, just to make sure they didn't hit anyone when they flew away.

Truth was, Ebony hated the idea of flying to the end of the rainbow. Who knew how far it would be? What if the rainbow went on forever? Okay, she knew it couldn't go on *forever*. But it could still be a very long flight and she could barely go a few feet without crashing.

"Ready?" Alistair asked with a bright smile.

"Yes?" Ebony hadn't meant her answer to sound like a question, but it did.

"Are you okay?" Alistair tilted his head as he looked closely at her.

"You know how I feel about flying," she whispered. Everyone at the academy had seen her fall at least once, if not a hundred times. She was a laughingstock two years in a row at Flying for Beginners and still dreaded the class.

"I know," Alistair said. "But don't worry. I'll be right here next to you. I'll help you the whole way."

Ebony felt a little better. Alistair had always been good at flying. Maybe he wasn't the most coordinated creature on the ground, but in the air, he was a whole different dragon.

"Come on!" Alistair held out his claw for Ebony's. With a deep breath, she took it and closed her eyes. "On the count of three, okay? One . . . two . . . three!"

With all her might, she flapped her wings and took off. She had barely gotten off the ground when the wind blew so hard that she lost her balance. Ailstair gripped her tighter and helped her steady herself.

"It's okay, you've got this!"

After a few moments, Ebony started to believe him. Maybe she *did* have this!

"You're doing great, Ebony!"

Ebony didn't want to open her eyes. She thought as soon as she did, she'd go crashing down to the ground below. But she also couldn't fly blindly, so she slowly opened one eye at a time.

Though she faltered a few times, Alistair never let her fall. He grabbed her talons tightly to keep her in the air until she caught her balance.

After ten minutes, they came to the end of the rainbow near a lake and landed.

"You did great!" Alistair gave her a nice, though hard, pat on the shoulder.

He definintely doesn't realize his own strength, Ebony thought as she wobbled from the force. She watched her friend, all smiles and laughs, as he looked out across the big lake they landed near.

"Alistair, can I ask you something?"

"Sure."

"How come you're so happy all the time? Others make jokes about your clumsiness and, well, you *are* kind of clumsy."

Alistair laughed again. She'd always admired that. It was one of the reasons she wanted to be friends with him in the first place.

Ebony, on the other hand, was always a little nervous around others. She knew everyone was thinking about how crazy it was that a griffin couldn't fly well.

"You have to focus on the good," Alistair said, looking at the rainbow above them. "Maybe you aren't the best flyer, but you are at the top of our Identifying Monsters and A History of Monstrology courses. You should focus on that—what you're good at—instead of what you're maybe not so good at."

Ebony smiled. "You know something? You're pretty smart, too, Alistair."

"I like to think so," he said with a big grin. "Now, let's look for that pot of gold!"

They searched all along the edge of the lake. The water was murky, so it was hard to see anything more than some rocks and some plants swaying beneath the water. Not long after they started searching, Alistair tripped. For a guy who made flying look easy, he really wasn't that great on the ground.

"Oh, Alistair," Ebony chuckled as she walked over to help him up.

He glanced back at what he had tripped on. "Hey, it's a pot! Do you think this is Declan's?" Alistair asked.

Ebony poked her head into it, but didn't see anything that showed it was Declan's. All she found inside of it was a pool of water and some plants. When Alistair picked it up to examine the plants closer, Ebony noticed that they looked exactly like the ones in the lake.

How strange! she thought.

"Let's look around a little longer," Alistair suggested. They searched the area where the pot was found until something glimmering near the lake caught Ebony's attention. When she went closer, she realized it was a piece of gold . . . with Declan's face on it! "Alistair, come see this!"

"Wow, real gold!" Alistair said. "I don't see any more around, do you?"

Ebony shook her head. "Maybe it's the only piece left behind. We should ask Declan when the last time it rained was. If it was recent, it would explain the water inside the pot. But if not . . . well, I don't know. Let's bring the plants, too, just in case they turn out to be a clue."

Alistair nodded and held out his free claw to her. With a deep breath, she took his claw and jumped up into the air.

CHAPTER SIX

FINDERS KEEPERS

Fiona didn't like being stuck at Declan's. Not. At. All. It smelled like rotting vegetables and the floorboards creaked whenever Declan walked around. Everything was a mess, too. His bed was unmade, his clothes were all over the floor, and his kitchen looked like everything had fallen out of the cabinets.

No wonder he's taking so long to make a cup of tea, she thought as she looked under the bed and inside some of the drawers. She even checked his kitchen cabinets, only to discover that's where Declan kept his toothbrush (and a lawn gnome for some odd reason).

When Fiona's searching turned up no clues, she huffed and sat down. Maybe her friends had found the gold at the end of some other rainbow where Declan had probably left it and forgot, like everyone in town was saying.

If not, Fiona wasn't really sure what to do next. Her friends were some of the smartest creatures at the academy, so she was sure they'd bring back the pot of gold—but should they? If someone came across his gold and took it, she was pretty sure that was within their rights. Finders keepers, after all. Wasn't that a thing with leprechauns' gold?

Declan set a bowl of tea down in front of Fiona, snapping her out of her thoughts. She eyed the bowl and lifted an eyebrow at Declan as she took a sip.

"Sorry, I still can't find any of my cups. I don't know where I put them. . . ."

"Maybe check under the sink in the bathroom," she said. When she had been searching, she was pretty sure she'd seen cups there.

"Oh, I'd never think to look there!" he said with a bright smile.

But apparently you'd think to put them there in the first place, Fiona thought as she took another sip of tea. It wasn't half bad, actually.

"You might have a messy house, Declan, but you sure do know how to make a good cup of tea," she said.

Declan beamed at the compliment. "Thanks! It's an old family recipe, the skin of a mushroom, lavender with a dash of honey, and a hint—only a hint!—of mud for that grit-in-your-mouth texture."

Fiona choked on her next sip. When Declan glanced away, she silently spat the tea back into the bowl.

"I'm sorry about my place," Declan muttered as he looked around. "There was a bad storm two weeks ago and the rain flooded it. I thought I was going to drown, honestly. I was going to get my roof and floors fixed so it doesn't happen again. But I can't pay for any of the repairs I need without my gold."

"Wait, is that why your home looks like this?" Fiona asked. "Because of the flood? We thought you were just sloppy."

Declan nodded. "I know, it's embarrassing . . . but I thought, what's the point in cleaning now? Without fixing the problems, it'll just get messed up when it rains again."

Fiona couldn't help it—she felt sorry for Declan. Maybe he wasn't the most organized creature, but no one deserved for their home to be flooded. She frowned as she looked at the droopy ceiling and mishappen, sticky floorboards.

Maybe finders keepers isn't right, Fiona thought.

CHAPTER SEVEN

THE BIG LIGHTBULB MOMENT

Gibbon and Yuri got back to Declan's place at the same time Alistair and Ebony did.

"We found something!" Gibbon said giddily.

Alistair threw his claws up in the air. "We did, too! Let's see if Fiona and Declan found any clues!"

Eagerly, they opened the door to the house, where they found Fiona pretending to sip away at a bowl of tea. It was a funny sight, Gibbon had to admit. The bowl was at least half her size, but she clearly had the strength to hold it up.

Note to self, don't make Fiona mad. She might be small, but she is mighty!

"You guys are back!" Fiona said happily as she flew off the couch. "Did you find anything?"

"We found a piece of Declan's gold in the lake," Gibbon said triumphantly as he held out the coin.

"That *is* my gold!" Declan called out. He rushed over and held it next to his head with a huge smile. "See? Looks just like me!"

Gibbon laughed. When Declan smiled like that, he did look just like the portrait on the piece of gold.

"And we found your pot! It was empty just like you said," Ebony said.

"But there was water inside of it and these plants," Alistair added, holding out his claws so everyone could see the seaweed-like plants.

"Water?" Fiona hummed. She glanced at Declan and asked, "It hasn't rained in two weeks, right?"

"That's right," Declan said. "Believe me, I'd know if it had."

"Two weeks is enough time for the water to have dried up by now," Ebony said. "That means the water is from something else. From something recent."

"Was the pot next to a lake or something?" Fiona asked.

"Yes, it was," Ebony replied. "There was a piece of his gold near it, too."

Gibbon had heard about people having lightbulb moments—when an idea clearly struck them and a lightbulb went off in their head—but this was the first time he ever saw it. Fiona's bright green eyes got even brighter somehow.

"So Yuri and Gibbon found some gold in the lake, and Alistair and Ebony found Declan's pot with lake plants in it. That's it! I think I know what happened! Back to the lake!" Fiona said.

When they got to the lake, Fiona, without saying a word to her friends, dove into the water—surprising everybody.

"Can she swim?" Gibbon asked nervously.

"I think so?" Ebony replied, but her voice didn't sound very certain.

"She's been down there a while. . . ." Yuri mumbled a bit anxiously.

Just as Gibbon was really starting to worry, Fiona emerged from the water with . . . a horse? Gibbon blinked hard a few times, making sure he was really seeing what he thought he was.

The horse trotted out of the water as Fiona flew over to the others. She stopped next to Gibbon and shook herself like a dog, splashing water all over him.

"Hey!"

"Sorry," Fiona laughed.

"What's a horse doing in the lake?" Yuri scratched his head as he looked the blue and green horse up and down.

"Oh, I know!" Ebony jumped with excitement. "You're a kelpie! They're a type of creature that lives in lakes—but wait, what are you doing in Ireland? Aren't kelpies from Scotland?"

"During the last storm, I got washed away from my family's loch," the kelpie said sadly. "The waves were so rough. When I finally woke up, I found myself near the shore here, far from home. I went to the first lake I could find. I couldn't find my way back, so I just stayed here."

"What's this have to do with my gold?" Declan asked, rubbing his beard.

"I figured it out from your clues," Fiona said, grinning. "You guys found a piece of Declan's gold in the lake. And then you two found the pot and the lake plants inside it, which got me thinking—what if the gold was *inside* the lake? But just too deep for anyone to see it? What if something inside the lake took it? There's tons of lore about lake creatures in these parts."

"Awesome job, Fiona!" Yuri pumped his fist in the air.

"You guys were the ones to find all the clues. I just put them together," she said with a smile and a shrug. She turned toward the kelpie. "What's your name? And why did you take Declan's gold?"

"My name is Lachlan, and I'm sorry," the kelpie said, lowering his head. "Back home, we have beautiful rocks and fish all around us. But this lake is dark and dreary. I thought that your gold was pretty and shiny, and could make the lake feel more like home. I didn't realize it belonged to someone."

Declan watched Lachlan for a long moment. Then, he walked over to the kelpie and smiled at him.

"Don't worry, friend," Declan said. "No harm done here. I'm sorry you got washed away from your family. That storm almost ruined my house, too. Everyone needs their home." Declan and Lachlan exchanged friendly, understanding smiles.

"I have an idea!" Yuri said as a grin grew wide across his face.

CHAPTER EIGHT

OVER AND OUT

The sea shimmered brightly as the sun set, turning the water a beautiful shade of orange and pink. *What a great day!* Yuri thought to himself.

He was proud of what he and his friends had accomplished. Declan stood near them, smiling as he watched his new friend, Lachlan the kelpie, run toward his loved ones. His family was a rainbow of colors as they waited for him on the far shore.

Yuri was good with maps. Always had been. He planned the route from Scotland to Ireland and back again easily, and Fiona then flew to Lachlan's loch in Scotland and led his family to their missing member.

We found Declan's gold AND reunited the kelpie family! Yuri wanted to shout to the whole world, but he kept it inside. This moment was for the kelpies to reunite.

"Well done, students," a voice said. Yuri turned to see Fitzgerald leaning against a nearby tree and smiling. "You solved not one case, but two. See how even the smallest details can be important?"

"We do," Gibbon said, nodding. "I'm really glad we were able to help Declan find his gold and also help the kelpie get home. I admit I thought this mission was a little . . . boring at first. But now I get it."

Alistair flapped his wings in excitement. "Can we have another mission, Fitzgerald? Please?"

Fitzgerald laughed. "You all have to get back to the academy, first. But since you did such a good job, I'll make sure to keep you all in mind the next time I hear about a mission."

Yuri looked at each of his friends. Gibbon and Alistair were laughing and goofing off. Fiona gave Ebony a thumbs-up. And for the first time in ages, Yuri saw that Ebony looked not only happy, but confident. He felt lucky to have each of them as a friend. Now that they were starting to believe in themselves, what mission *wouldn't* they be able to solve?

Isle of
MISFITS
PRANK WARS!

BOOK 3

I SMELL

by JAMIE MAE   illustrated by FREYA HARTAS

READ ON FOR A SNEAK PE
FROM THE THIRD BOOK IN T
ISLE OF MISFITS SERI

CHAPTER ONE

A BABA YAGA, A TROLL, A GHOUL, AND A GREMLIN GET A MISSION

"**W**e just got the coolest mission ever!"

Gibbon stopped walking when he heard someone talking about missions. Gibbon and his friends went on their first mission to help another creature a month ago, and he couldn't wait to go on another one! Who else could have gotten a mission?

When he turned to look, he saw Lissa, the baba yaga, in the center of a big group of classmates. He had just left his History of Cursed Jewels class with his friends. Even though they all stood on the steps of the school building, he seemed to be the only one who heard Lissa. Ebony, Fiona, and Yuri chatted about what they'd learned in class while Alistair nodded along.

Gibbon stepped a little closer to Lissa to hear what she was saying better.

"What do you get to do?" a harpy asked, flapping her birdish arms around excitedly.

"It's top secret," Lissa said as she folded her arms and grinned.

"He said he couldn't trust anyone else with this!" added Gashsnarl the ghoul with a high five to Trom.

Gibbon rolled his eyes. *Maybe* they were telling the truth, but he remembered how their team acted during the obstacle course race a few months ago. Gibbon's team came in second place in the competition, but still won because Fitzgerald saw Lissa trip Gibbon at the very end. If they were playing fair and square, Gibbon was sure he and his friends would have won.

Why would Fitzgerald give them a secret mission? Gibbon wondered. So what if Lissa and Gashsnarl were some of the top students in their class, coming second only to Ebony? They were cheaters.

"What's wrong?" Yuri asked, nudging Gibbon.

"Lissa's bragging about a secret mission," he muttered.

Yuri frowned as he looked over at

the crowd surrounding Gashsnarl and Lissa. "Really? *They* got a mission? How come we didn't get another mission?"

"We helped Declan not too long ago," Ebony said.

Gibbon looked to Yuri and knew his friend was thinking the exact same thing as him. Helping Declan the leprechaun find his gold had been *so* long ago. Since then, all they'd been doing was going to classes, classes, and more classes. He loved learning about so many new things, but he longed for the adventure of another mission, probably just as much as Yuri did.

Alistair sighed. "I do miss helping other creatures. Remember how happy Declan was when we found his gold?

That was cool."

"Lissa is just being a show-off, like always," Fiona said as she flapped her wings with attitude.

"Since we don't have a mission, shouldn't we focus on school?" Ebony asked. She held up her stack of textbooks. "We have an exam coming up next week in the Art of Bewitching."

Reluctantly, Gibbon nodded. His favorite part about being on the Isle of Misfits was all the books he got to read at the library. Their collection was so much bigger than the one at the castle he grew up in. His least favorite part of the isle was tests, but with Ebony's help, he knew he'd usually pass them.

With one final look back at Lissa and Gashsnarl, Gibbon went with his friends to the ivy-covered library.

JAMIE MAE is a children's book author living in Brooklyn with her fluffy dog, Boo. Before calling New York home, she lived in Quebec, Australia, and France. She loves learning about monsters, mysteries, and mythologies from all around the globe.

⟷

FREYA HARTAS is a UK-based illustrator specializing in children's books. She lives in the vibrant city of Bristol and works from her cozy, cluttered desk. Freya loves to conjure up humorous characters, animals, and monsters and to create fantastical worlds and places for them to inhabit and get lost in.

Journey to some magical places and outer space, rock out, and find your inner superhero with these other chapter book series from **Little Bee Books!**

little bee books
an imprint of Bonnier Publishing USA